"Three cheer[...] Young readers [...] know this love[ly, bright] young lady. Annabelle has a strong self-esteem and her positivity is contagious. Linda Taylor has done a wonderful job of creating a character for young readers to look up to and aspire to be like.

"Annabelle handles adversity with integrity and wisdom. Readers will gain priceless life lessons from the Amazing Annabelle Series. These books are heart-warming, entertaining, and a treat for readers of all ages."
—*Meredith Szypot, 4th Grade Teacher*

"The books so well present real situations in which students find themselves in terms of inter-relationships with one another. They acknowledge their feelings and work through them.

"The books are an easy read with strong vocabulary and wonderful family nuances. I love the wholesomeness of the books."
—*Mary Rettaliatta, Asst. Superintendent*

Amazing Annabelle
THANK YOU, VETERANS!

LINDA TAYLOR
ILLUSTRATED BY KYLE HORNE

Lightswitch
LEARNING
a Sussman Education company

250 East 54th Street, P2
New York, NY 10022

www.lightswitchlearning.com

Educators and Librarians, for a variety of teaching resources, visit
www.lightswitchlearning.com

ISBN: 978-1-94782901-5

Printed in China

To my countless

students—

Oh, how you've

inspired me!

Contents

Thank You, Veterans

What's new in Social Studies?
A new unit for Veterans Day.
Trips, projects, recognition, fun,
and celebrations are underway.

Drama Club is starting up
Interesting activities and exercises
take place.
Ideas and decisions are brewing.
Annabelle always speaks up
and defends her case.

1

DRAMA CLUB

November was always a great time of the year for Annabelle Copeland. It was a time of giving extra thanks. Annabelle and her mom would often volunteer at a senior home and help the people who lived there to play Bingo and various board games.

Once Annabelle spent one whole Saturday making special happy face cards to pass out to all the seniors. She decorated them with markers, tissue paper, and stickers. She also wrote a special message inside of every card. No one told her to do this, she just wanted to spread joy and see the smiles on everyone's faces.

Annabelle had so many leftover cards that she started passing out the rest to all the nurses and other workers. That's just the kind of amazing person Annabelle is. Sharing and doing for others is a top priority for her.

Mrs. Mitchell, her teacher, was planning two big units in Social Studies this month. The class was going to do one on the Native Americans and Pilgrims, and another one on the veterans of this country. Annabelle loved all subjects across the board, but these monthly units were very special and exciting.

Mrs. Mitchell said that there would be a lot of role-playing involved this time. What Mrs. Mitchell didn't know was that Annabelle was a natural born actress extraordinaire, at least in her own imagination. Annabelle and her friend Kaitlyn would often put together make-believe scenes which they would act out at her house, so role-playing was right up Annabelle's alley.

Not only would Annabelle be able to do role-playing in class, but she also could role-play in Drama Club, which would be starting in a week. She and Kaitlyn just saw a big sign hanging up near the cafeteria about it.

"Oh my goodness! I can't believe this! My time has really arrived! I'll finally be able to act on the stage right here at Melville School!" Annabelle said with excitement.

"You and me both! We'll be a complete hit!" Kaitlyn matched her enthusiasm.

There was a sign-up sheet next to the poster, and they both signed it immediately.

"They must have just put this sign up since we are the first and second names on the list," Annabelle said.

"I wonder who's going to teach the drama class," Kaitlyn said.

"I don't know, but I hope they're really good and can recognize pure talent when they see it," Annabelle replied.

"You got that right, sister! I'll have to remember to bring my sunglasses on the first day of the club," Kaitlyn said and they both laughed.

Just then Victoria came walking by and noticed Annabelle and Kaitlyn pretending to be actresses near the poster. Victoria was in their class and didn't care too much for either of them.

Annabelle thought Victoria liked to brag and was prideful at times, but Annabelle still tried to be friendly towards her anyway.

"I see you two have signed up for the Drama Club," Victoria said to them. "I was going to sign up earlier, but I had to go and get a pencil. I didn't realize you were into stuff like that. Oh well, I guess anyone can get into a club these days. I'll see you two at the first meeting then. Tootles!"

Victoria didn't even give them a chance to answer back before she walked away, not that they would anyway.

"That's it. I'm taking my name off the list!" Kaitlyn groaned, fumbling for her pencil.

"You will do no such thing!" Annabelle snapped. "You can't let Victoria get to you like that. We're joining together so just forget about her."

"How can I forget about her when she's going to be at all the club meetings with us?" Kaitlyn asked.

"We'll just have to tune her out and pay her no mind. Besides, we're going to be having such a good time, we'll barely notice her." Annabelle tried to encourage her friend.

"Okay. But if she starts to get on my nerves, I'm just going to leave," Kaitlyn warned.

"Either we'll both fight the good fight together or we'll both leave," Annabelle said firmly.

"And what exactly does 'tootles' mean anyway?" Kaitlyn wondered.

"It's a fancy way to say goodbye, I think."

"Then why doesn't she just say bye?" Kaitlyn asked.

"We both know Victoria is way too fancy for that." The girls laughed.

"Maybe we should just call her Queen Victoria and bow to her highness whenever we see her," Kaitlyn joked, changing her voice to sound like an English lady.

"Knowing her, she'd probably like us to do that." Annabelle replied. "But I would never give her that satisfaction, and neither should you—not even joking around."

"I guess you're right about that," Kaitlyn agreed.

"Hey, why don't you come over to my house after school, and we can brush up on our acting techniques," Annabelle suggested.

"Sure thing! I think I have some great new props we could use to stage a scene!"

Annabelle and Kaitlyn hurried outside to catch their bus.

2

VETERANS UNIT ASSIGNMENT

Since Veterans Day is on November 11th, Mrs. Mitchell's class worked on the Veterans Unit first. Mrs. Mitchell really wanted her students to get a better understanding of veterans in general, the work they've done for our country, and how many of them live their lives. She shared the first assignment with her class.

"Next week our class will be going on a special field trip to a Veterans Recreational Center," Mrs. Mitchell began. "We're going to be interviewing veterans and getting to know these really special people a little better. I want you to work in groups and come up with about five specific questions we can ask them in the interview," Mrs. Mitchell instructed.

This assignment was really near and dear to Annabelle's heart because her grandpa was a veteran. She remembered stories he would tell of going overseas and serving in his army unit. Annabelle's dad told her that Grandpa was a war hero and received a Purple Heart medal for being wounded in action. Her grandpa lives in a nursing home now, but Annabelle and her family visit him each month.

Every time Mrs. Mitchell divided the class into groups for one of these special assignments, one thing she always did was shuffle them around so that they were made up of completely different students than the time before. Some of the groups were made up of students who would never choose to be in the same group, but for some odd reason that's what Mrs. Mitchell did.

Of course, there was always a method to her madness. Mrs. Mitchell loved to observe students spending time together and see if unexpected friendships formed. She wanted to see who the leaders, talkers, followers, and quiet students were.

Mrs. Mitchell also wanted to see what made certain students either come alive or shut down in discussions. She knew some combinations of certain students would always work together and do well. But she wondered what the results would be if students got mixed up a bit. A lot of surprises were about to happen.

Annabelle was placed in a group with Kara, Jake, Tyler, and Victoria. Kara was quiet most of the time and never caused a problem. Jake and Tyler were often talkative in a negative way and sometimes bullies. They would often get on each other's nerves, and many times got each other in trouble by tattling.

And Victoria . . . Just the other day, Annabelle had an unpleasant time with Victoria, where she acted like a snob in

Drama Club. Needless to say, Annabelle wasn't pleased with Victoria being in her group, but she wasn't going to let that stop her from getting the most out of this assignment. She was going to do her job to the best of her ability.

Annabelle immediately opened her notebook and took on the job of recorder. Annabelle was a natural born leader and put herself in charge right away. She just couldn't help it. Her mom said she was wired that way.

"So, does anyone have any good questions they would ask a veteran?" Annabelle began.

Not one person in her group spoke up to say anything. Annabelle wasn't expecting that at all. *Did they not hear the question that was just asked?* After a short silence, Tyler raised his hand to speak.

Grateful for some interest, Annabelle

said, "Tyler, you really don't have to raise your hand, just say it."

"What is a veteran?" Tyler asked.

"Stop kidding around, Tyler, or else I'm going to tell Mrs. Mitchell!" Jake warned his friend.

"I'm not kidding! I really don't know!" Tyler admitted, embarrassed.

"Were you *not* listening to Mrs. Mitchell before she gave us this assignment? She already explained it to us!" Victoria demanded.

"Fine! I won't ask any more questions then!" Tyler was angry now.

Annabelle saw the disappointment in Tyler's eyes and kindly got involved in the conversation.

"A veteran is a person who has served or is serving in the armed forces military," explained Annabelle. "My own grandpa is actually a veteran," she was proud to say.

"Really? Why did he want to go into the military? He could've gotten injured or even died!" Tyler pointed out.

"Actually, Tyler, you have just given us our first question for our assignment, which is, 'Why did you want to go into the military?'" Annabelle said as she quickly wrote down the first question.

"That's a good question, Tyler," Kara said quietly.

"Who has another question for our list? Just think of something you might ask an old person," Annabelle suggested.

"I don't speak with old people, and I really wouldn't know what to say to them," Victoria declared. "We don't have anything in common, and we don't even like the same things!"

Annabelle asked in the kindest way

she could, "How would you even know that if you don't ask? I think Victoria has just given us our second question, which is, 'What are some of the things you like in this world?'"

"Whatever you say, Annabelle. I guess you're in charge of this little group thing anyway," Victoria grumbled.

Annabelle wasn't sure if Victoria was saying her comment in a positive or negative manner, but she didn't let it bother her. She was very focused on the assignment and was just happy to be coming up with questions even though the group got a slow start. As they continued to loosen up and become more vocal, both Kara and Jake came up with good questions as well.

Annabelle already had so many questions to ask in her head. She really could've done this assignment by herself, but just like Mrs. Mitchell, she likes to involve others in whatever task she does.

Annabelle's dad would always tell her that everyone's voice is important and meaningful, even if you don't agree with it.

It turned out to be a pretty good group after all, even with Victoria.

3

FIRST DRAMA CLUB MEETING

Annabelle was very excited about the first Drama Club meeting after school. Although she and Kaitlyn would put on a show at their homes from time to time, she wondered if this was going to be the real thing. *Then again, acting is not real, it's make-believe,* Annabelle thought. She really hoped this club would be a lot of fun, and she was about to find out.

Mrs. Phillips, the lunch monitor, was the teacher for the Drama Club. During the day, she helped out in the cafeteria and watched the kids during recess. Mrs.

Phillips was always so friendly to all the students, but she was also very firm when she needed to be. She could just give students a certain look, and they would stop fooling around in the cafeteria. She reminded Annabelle of a spunky young lady who had a lot of energy.

About fifteen students attended the first drama club meeting after school. Many students were very surprised to see Mrs. Phillips, especially Victoria.

"Mrs. Phillips, what are you doing here? Where is the drama teacher?" Victoria demanded.

"I'm the drama teacher, and I'm glad to see you too. Please take a seat so we can get started," Mrs. Phillips said smiling.

Victoria wondered what a lunch monitor could possibly know about acting. She seemed to get herself a little upset before the meeting even began.

But Annabelle's mom had told her to never judge people before knowing anything about them. She always said that you just have to get to know them a little better, and they may surprise you.

It seemed to Annabelle that Mrs. Phillips might have lots of hidden talents that many students didn't even know about yet, and the group would certainly find out soon.

When all the students were sitting down, Mrs. Phillips took the stage and did a three-minute dramatic speech and then sang a short song! The students later found out the speech and song were from the Broadway play *Annie*.

Afterwards all the students stood up and clapped for her because they were really impressed, even Victoria.

"Now, let me properly introduce myself. My name is Mrs. Patty Phillips, and

I will be your Drama Club teacher for the school year. In this class, we're going to play a lot of acting games and get to know each other really well. It's very possible that we may act out a series of short skits to perform right here at Melville School, if everything goes well. Now does anyone have any questions for me before we get started?" Mrs. Phillips asked.

Annabelle quickly raised her hand with excitement and asked, "Where did you learn how to sing and act like that?"

"I started taking singing, dancing, and acting lessons at a very early age. I practiced a lot and was in quite a few productions in my day," Mrs. Phillips said.

"So, were you ever rich and famous? Do you know any movie stars now? And what are you doing with yourself these days?" Victoria blurted out.

Many students began to laugh at Victoria's questions and talk quietly with each other about them so Mrs. Phillips wouldn't hear.

Annabelle thought Victoria's last question was out of line and spoke up boldly, "I can't believe you asked that last question, Victoria! Obviously, she's working with kids like us, teaching us all about drama!"

"She did say we could ask her questions. I don't know why you're getting so upset, Annabelle," Victoria said quickly.

Mrs. Phillips didn't seem to be bothered by Victoria's questions at all but instead graciously responded.

"I will gladly answer all your questions. I never reached superstar status in the acting business, so I was never rich or very famous. I did know quite a few movie stars, but we don't keep in touch," she explained and then paused for a minute.

"And as for what I'm doing with myself these days," Mrs. Phillips continued,

"I'm enjoying working with terrific young people. Little do you know it, but you keep me young at heart as well."

Annabelle thought Mrs. Phillips was one classy lady. She certainly wasn't going to let a disrespectful comment get to her. Mrs. Phillips had a job to do, and she was going to carry it out no matter what people thought about her.

Annabelle gained a high opinion of Mrs. Phillips in just one session, as many others did as well. She couldn't wait to see how this Drama Club was going to unfold.

After all the pre-drama activity, the actual class went on without a hitch. Mrs. Phillips included an awesome get-to-know-you game that had everyone introducing a different person in the club. The only catch was that they had to introduce the person in a different voice from their own original voice. If the person left out any information about who they were introducing, the person could jump in and add more information.

The kids were all laughing and having a good time, even Victoria. They were really learning a lot about each other in a fun way.

The Drama Club seemed to be off to a good start.

4

ANNABELLE'S IDEAS

During the next day in school, Annabelle had an amazing idea for the Veterans Unit they were working on in Social Studies. Once Annabelle took a liking to a theme or topic of interest, her mind would go into overdrive, allowing her creative juices to flow freely. She just couldn't help herself. Annabelle always thought on a large scale and wanted the creative ideas she had to reach others and make them happy.

Before the lesson started, Annabelle excitedly approached Mrs. Mitchell's desk to share her ideas privately.

"Mrs. Mitchell, I wanted to know if the whole class could make some really cool thank-you cards for the Veterans before we go on our trip next week."

Mrs. Mitchell nodded her head. "I think that's a great idea!" she said. "I know receiving those cards would definitely put an extra smile on their faces."

Annabelle continued, "Maybe we could sing some patriotic songs too, like 'Grand Old Flag' and 'America' and 'This Land Is Your Land,'" she suggested.

"I don't know if the class knows these songs super well right now," Mrs. Mitchell said with a slight frown.

"We could definitely learn them!" said Annabelle. "We're all fast learners!"

"But we're going next week," reminded Mrs. Mitchell, "and we might not have the time to go over them."

She tried to calm Annabelle down gently. "Let's just wait on that idea for now. Maybe we can learn the songs for another time."

Annabelle was thrilled that Mrs. Mitchell agreed with even one of her ideas. She decided that maybe her teacher figured that singing was just pushing the envelope a little too much for now.

However, she didn't let this get her down.

When Mrs. Mitchell began the lesson, she made sure to announce to the class that Annabelle had come up with the great idea to make thank-you cards for the Veterans. After the lesson, Mrs. Mitchell left time for the class to make the cards.

"This was a really great idea, Annabelle," said Kaitlyn. "I just love doing arts and crafts. And we get to do it during class time!"

"Yeah, we could be doing harder reading or writing work, but instead we're just making some silly cards," Todd said, joking.

Of course that comment didn't sit well with Annabelle at all.

"This is so much more than a silly as-signment, Todd," she explained. "We're all taking part in an important task by creating these meaningful cards to bring joy to a bunch of great veterans who have served our country well."

Kaitlyn agreed, saying, "That's right, it may be an easy assignment, but doing this has a deeper purpose that you need to understand."

"Okay, okay. I didn't mean to offend anyone. I was just speaking my mind. Sorry, all right?" Todd said, wanting to be forgiven after he better understood what it was all about.

"You know, you're right, Annabelle. My uncle is a veteran. I think I'm going to make a card for him too," Todd said.

"Now that's the spirit! I wonder how many other students have relatives who are veterans?" Kaitlyn said.

Another idea just popped into Annabelle's mind.

"That's a very good question, Kaitlyn. Maybe we should ask the class. Or better yet, ask the whole school!" Annabelle said with excitement.

"How will we do that, Annabelle?" Kaitlyn asked.

"Before I say anything else, I better run it by Mrs. Mitchell. This idea is really big!" Annabelle exclaimed and quickly went to Mrs. Mitchell's desk again.

"Mrs. Mitchell, I have one more big idea. What would you think of asking the class or even the whole school to see who has veterans in their families? Then maybe we could invite them in and have a special celebration for them in the school," Annabelle asked excitedly.

Mrs. Mitchell thought about the idea before she spoke.

"You know, Annabelle, you might be on to something here. I was thinking about doing some kind of school project, and this might just be it. Let me ask Principal Jefferson to see if it's possible. I'll let you know soon."

Annabelle was on cloud nine. She couldn't believe that her big idea might actually be a schoolwide project! Maybe they could include singing the patriotic songs in the program! This could be the major event of the month! She couldn't wait to hear back from Mrs. Mitchell.

5

DRAMA, DRAMA

Annabelle's mind was still reeling from Social Studies class earlier as she and Kaitlyn went to Drama Club.

"You know, Kaitlyn, I just want to thank you for sparking my big idea earlier about the veteran's celebration. I really think it might happen," Annabelle said.

"Listen, any time I can be a part of your big ideas is a plus in my life," Kaitlyn assured her. "Besides, I know we'll have a great time putting things together with Mrs. Mitchell and maybe even the principal!"

Annabelle could only hope that would be the case.

That day in drama class Mrs. Phillips started off with all the students doing some relaxation exercises. She said the more you relax your mind and body, the more you'll be able to focus your attention on something else.

She asked everyone to lay on the stage and pretend they were on a blanket at the beach. She wanted the students to pretend to hear the sounds of the waves crashing in their ears in the cool, peaceful, and calm atmosphere.

As everyone took deep breaths and loosened up, some students really became super relaxed—some a little more than others. Several minutes into the exercise, the class started to hear some loud snoring. It turned out to be Tyler, who had fallen asleep on the floor!

Some of the students immediately noticed Tyler and came out of their relaxed state with lots of giggles. Mrs. Phillips went over to Tyler and gently nudged him on the shoulder to wake him up. Startled, Tyler jumped up with his eyes wide open. He noticed everyone staring at him.

"Good morning. Was I snoring again?" Tyler asked, smiling.

At that point everyone was in full laughter mode. Mrs. Phillips had to get the students under control.

"Okay, settle down, everyone. Sleepy heads will prevail from time to time. I'm sure Tyler has had a long and tiresome day," Mrs. Phillips said, taking Tyler's side.

"Or maybe he was just bored with this activity," said Victoria.

Once again, Annabelle couldn't believe the rude jabs that came out of Victoria's mouth. Annabelle thought Victoria was so disrespectful, especially to Mrs. Phillips.

Once again, Annabelle had to speak her peace. "I really don't think Tyler was bored, Victoria. This happens to be a great warm-up and relaxing exercise.

Maybe Tyler just didn't get enough sleep last night."

"I did try to stay up late to watch that final wrestle mania match," he said in his defense. "It was so awesome! Cameron the Krusher was beating Barry the Beast, but then I fell asleep on the couch and didn't get to watch the ending. It must have been past eleven p.m., easy."

"Well, maybe it was just me that was bored," Victoria said in not a very nice tone of voice.

Kaitlyn had enough of Victoria and said, "The class has just started. We have only been here for about ten minutes. If you're bored, Victoria, why don't you just quit the club and stop coming?"

It just so happened that many of the other students didn't like Victoria's earlier statements and were feeling the same way as Kaitlyn. Multiple students started agreeing with Kaitlyn's statement. This upset Victoria even more.

"None of you are the boss of me, so I don't have to listen to any of you!" Victoria shouted.

Mrs. Phillips quickly interrupted the heated conversation. "Listen, no one is leaving drama class. We must have an open mind about exercises, be patient, and just let things happen. A bigger purpose is always behind even the simplest of things."

"I'm leaving any way. I know when I'm not wanted." Victoria gathered her things and stormed out.

One would think Victoria loved drama so much that she would never think of quitting, considering the performance she just gave. Annabelle started to feel bad about the whole situation.

"This is certainly *not* what I expected

for our second drama class!" said Mrs. Phillips sadly. "We have to respect others, even if they're different from us or we don't like something about their personality. We don't always have to agree with the way things are done or said, but we do have to respect others."

Annabelle thought Mrs. Phillips sounded a little like her mom, and what she said really made sense to her. Victoria certainly had a not-so-great personality. Maybe she was good at other things. Some people just need direction or a real friend to calmly show them gentler and kinder ways of relating to others.

Or maybe something was really bothering Victoria deep inside, Annabelle wondered. She remembered that her mom always said all situations happened for a reason. Maybe this whole thing had just been a very big misunderstanding.

Annabelle felt the need to have a real heart-to-heart talk with Victoria. But would Victoria even allow it? Would she even talk to Annabelle? Would Victoria listen to her and take her seriously? Annabelle realized that there was only one way to find out.

6

ANNABELLE'S IDEAS PREVAIL

The next day at school, Annabelle was called to the principal's office first thing in the morning. She wondered what on earth she did to get this uncommon invitation. Annabelle was an A+ student and very active in the school, so she knew it wasn't anything related to academics or discipline.

She became a little nervous as she walked down the long hallway. She wondered if it were family related or if anyone was hurt. All sorts of thoughts raced through Annabelle's mind all at once.

When she arrived, she saw her teacher sitting in the office along with Mr. Jefferson.

"Oh, Annabelle, come in. We were expecting you," Mr. Jefferson said, welcoming her into the office.

"Am I in trouble or something? Usually

kids only come to the principal's office when they're in trouble or if something bad has happened," Annabelle said quickly.

"Really? Those are the only reasons? Then starting next week I'm going to start inviting groups of students to my office for good behavior too," Mr. Jefferson said with a smile.

"Well, that's a great idea, Mr. Jefferson!" Annabelle said in a relieved tone.

Mrs. Mitchell looked surprised and then smiled too.

"We're going to hold you to that statement, Mr. Jefferson. And I too think it's a great idea," Mrs. Mitchell said.

"So then why am I here?" Annabelle asked, looking around.

"I was told by Mrs. Mitchell that you

came up with a great idea for our veterans. Can you share your idea with me?" he asked.

"Oh sure, Mr. Jefferson! I was thinking that we could find out which students have a veteran in their family and then have a special celebration for them here at Melville School!" Annabelle said with excitement.

"I think that's a magnificent idea," said Mr. Jefferson. "I would like you and Mrs. Mitchell and your entire class to organize this grand event. Do you think you'd be able to put this together?" Mr. Jefferson asked.

"Absolutely! Mrs. Mitchell could head up this project, and then we could organize groups and use a lot of teamwork!" Annabelle replied without a second thought.

"I like the sound of that, and I like

your spirit, Annabelle. I know this project is in good hands," declared Mr. Jefferson.

Mrs. Mitchell looked as if she agreed and seemed to love the plans for what was going to happen. Annabelle was bursting with excitement as she and Mrs. Mitchell left Mr. Jefferson's office.

A few questions came to Annabelle's mind so she began to question Mrs. Mitchell as they walked down the hall together. "So, how are we going to start things off, Mrs. Mitchell?"

"First, I think we should outline a plan of action and then see how we can best carry it out," Mrs. Mitchell answered.

"That sounds like a good strategy, Mrs. Mitchell. Are you going to do that as our lesson for today?" Annabelle asked.

"Absolutely, because we have no time to waste."

Mrs. Mitchell was absolutely right. They had about seven days to plan this if they wanted to do it on Veterans Day.

"Are you sure we're going to have enough time to pull everything together so quickly?" Annabelle questioned her teacher.

"I'm not too sure, but we can definitely do our best," Mrs. Mitchell assured her.

This would be a very big undertaking, and time would be an important factor. Maybe they would need more time to really pull this off well. Annabelle kept thinking and thinking about it all.

When they arrived in the classroom and told everyone what had happened in the principal's office, the class all clapped their hands. Mrs. Mitchell immediately started working on a plan by writing an outline on the board.

Now that Annabelle was seeing her

idea unfold, she really began to think that they would need more time to pull things together before Veterans Day. Just then, Annabelle had another idea. She didn't even speak to Mrs. Mitchell about it privately first. She just raised her hand and when she was recognized by her teacher, she spoke.

"Mrs. Mitchell, do we really have to have this program on Veterans Day? What if we combine it with our Thanksgiving activities and do it a few days before Thanksgiving?" Annabelle suggested.

"Yeah, then we could have a Veterans Thanksgiving Celebration!" Kaitlyn added.

Mrs. Mitchell thought about this idea for a minute as the class gave their input on this suggestion.

"I think that's a great idea because it

combines both holidays in a positive way," Jamal said.

"I think we should celebrate each holiday separately because they stand for different things," Jeanie said.

"We can still celebrate the holidays separately in school. We just want to have this celebration for the veterans as a token of our thankfulness to them. And it just so happens that we're doing it near Thanksgiving time," Annabelle explained.

"I think it's a great idea, and it gives the class more time to plan and prepare," Lila said.

"Also, they already have celebrations on Veterans Day for the veterans," Barry reminded them. "They have a big parade down Main Street where the mayor gives a speech, and they serve dinner for the veterans at the Civic Center."

"I think we should keep the celebration for veterans on Veterans Day and stop trying to change things around all the time," Victoria said.

To Annabelle, for some reason Victoria's response seemed as if it were aimed only at her in a mean way. But Annabelle didn't let that bother her at all.

Mrs. Mitchell decided to put the suggestion to a vote.

"All in favor of doing the celebration a few days before Thanksgiving Day, raise your hand," Mrs. Mitchell instructed.

Everyone raised their hand except two students, Jeanie and Victoria. So Annabelle's idea was a winner.

Mrs. Mitchell invited a small group of students to join her for an early meeting the next morning before class started to help discuss some ideas to present to the others.

Annabelle and Kaitlyn were in the special planning group. Mrs. Mitchell asked everyone to bring some ideas to the table. And that's exactly what Annabelle and Kaitlyn were going to do.

7

ANNABELLE TO THE RESCUE

Annabelle really had a lot of preparation to do after school today. She and Kaitlyn were going to sit down together and write down some ideas for the Veterans Thanksgiving Celebration to share in class tomorrow.

But first they had to go to their Drama Club practice. Annabelle was faithful to the club and wouldn't miss a day, even if she had extra homework to do.

As Annabelle was heading to drama class, she saw Victoria walking toward the door to catch the bus home. Annabelle took a chance and yelled to her to get her attention.

"Hey, Victoria, where are you going? Drama Club is this way," Annabelle said.

"I'm not doing Drama Club anymore, remember?" Victoria sounded sad.

"Look, you can't let every little thing get to you like that. You might not like all the exercises or activities that we do, but just try them and be open to them, and you might discover you actually enjoy them," Annabelle said.

"I don't know if you noticed, but no one really likes me in the club," Victoria said quietly.

Annabelle was surprised to hear Victoria expressing herself in this way. Victoria had always tried to look strong on the outside so that no one got to know how she was really feeling inside.

Annabelle remembered a conversation she had with her mom a while ago. She had told her that sometimes people put on a mask to cover how they're feeling inside. People can really be hurting or going through a lot of troubles in life, but they don't want anyone to know. They just get used to pretending and making things look good on the outside.

Annabelle's mom told her that she should always try to be extra nice to these people whenever she could and to try and get to know the real person inside.

Maybe Victoria just needed a friend to talk to sometimes. Annabelle decided at that moment to try and be that friend.

"I think some students will really miss you if you don't show up, Victoria. You have a lot of energy, and you bring a lot of drama to the Drama Club already. I think everyone is always excited and waiting to see what you're going to do next," Annabelle said.

Victoria thought about Annabelle's words. She had never thought of herself as being a person that others watched so closely. That very thought put a slight smile on Victoria's face and changed her attitude.

"My exit the other day was sort of dramatic, I guess. Maybe I should make another grand appearance today. One thing I do love is drama. I do it so well, don't you think?" Victoria said with new confidence.

"Oh, we all think you do, Victoria. Drama Club is a place for you to exercise your talent!" Annabelle said.

"I guess you talked me into it, Annabelle. I'll go to Drama Club today!" Victoria said.

Victoria turned around and walked toward the auditorium.

"I hope I don't regret this," Annabelle whispered to herself.

When Victoria got to the auditorium, everyone was so surprised to see her, just as she expected.

Mrs. Phillips greeted her with open arms, giving her a big hug. No teacher had ever hugged Victoria like that. She felt a warm feeling inside that she had not felt in a long time. She really liked it and smiled. It seemed as if the warm hug toned down her pride a bit. Victoria couldn't believe that Mrs. Phillips was actually happy to see her with all of the attitude she had given her.

"We're so happy to see you back, Victoria. I hope I can count on you to help us with some improvisations for today's class," Mrs. Phillips said.

"Of course, you can, Mrs. Phillips. I'd be delighted," Victoria said with a smile.

"Excuse me," said Tyler. "What exactly are improvisations anyway? I've never heard of them."

"I'm so glad you asked!" said Mrs Phillips. Improvisations are unplanned performances without any practice at all! Victoria and I are going to show you. Now, Victoria, I want you to pretend to be a customer in a restaurant, and I just accidentally spilled a tray of food on you. Are you ready?" Mrs. Phillips asked her.

Without thinking twice, Victoria nodded her head, jumped on the stage, and sat in a chair.

"Mrs. Phillips, can I be the waitress?" Annabelle quickly asked.

"You sure can. Now you two show the class how it's done."

Annabelle pretended to have a tray of food and spilled it on Victoria, the customer.

"Oh, madam, I'm so sorry! Let me try to clean you up!" Annabelle said.

"I can't believe you spilled this food on my new clothes! Now I'm going to be late for my very important meeting! How dare you! Where is your manager?" Victoria demanded.

"Oh, please madam, don't call my manager or else I'll get fired!" Annabelle pleaded. "Please forgive me!"

Really getting into her part, Victoria shouted, "Who is going to pay for my clothes? This outfit cost five-hundred dollars! Who is going to pay for it?"

"I don't have any money!" said Annabelle quietly. "But I could wash it out for you."

"Manager! Manager! I need to speak to a manager!" Victoria yelled.

Mrs. Phillips walked up to the stage

and stopped the improvisation skit.

"Okay now," she said, "that was some great improvisation! Give them both a hand of applause!"

The entire class clapped and was clearly very excited. They really enjoyed what they saw. Annabelle and Victoria each took a bow.

"Now aren't you glad you came to Drama Club today?" Annabelle asked Victoria.

"I sure am," Victoria exclaimed in happiness.

Everyone had a great time doing improvisations for the rest of the class, especially Victoria and Annabelle.

8

PLANNING SESSION

Annabelle and Kaitlyn were really starting to enjoy the Drama Club. They both had fun doing the improvisations.

"I can't believe Victoria actually came back," said Kaitlyn. "I thought she was gone forever."

"I actually had a little talk with her after school. I felt so bad that she stormed out of class the other day. I really thought that she should give it a second chance," Annabelle explained.

"I know you must have worked your magic on her. She seemed pleasant today and was easy to get along with. Her attitude wasn't too bad either," Kaitlyn said.

"All Victoria needed was a little hug and to feel loved. Mrs. Phillips certainly gave her that today. I think Victoria really likes to be included in activities," Annabelle decided. "She also loves being put on the spot so she can display her talents, which is exactly what Mrs. Phillips did."

"I hope this is the start of many more good days for Victoria," Kaitlyn said. "She was a totally different person today. Whatever you did was a blessing to her. Keep up the good work, Annabelle!"

After drama class, Kaitlyn went over to Annabelle's house to discuss plans for the Veterans Thanksgiving Celebration. Annabelle asked her mom to join them in the planning session.

"Okay, the first thing we have to do is

find out who has a veteran in their family."

"But how are we going to do that?" Annabelle asked.

"Maybe Mrs. Mitchell can send a letter home with all the students asking the parents. If they do have a family member who's a veteran, they can write

their names down on the letter and return it to school," Mrs. Copeland suggested.

"Mrs. Copeland, you are awesome!" said Kaitlyn. "That's a great idea! Maybe you can type a letter up for us!" Kaitlyn was excited.

"I think your teacher should type up the letter on the school letterhead so it's official. And she'll know exactly what to say," said Annabelle's mom. "I'm just here to give you two some assistance when needed."

Annabelle wrote the ideas in her notebook to show to Mrs. Mitchell tomorrow.

"Okay, maybe we should have the students who have veterans in their families introduce them! I can't wait to introduce my grandpa to everyone," Annabelle said.

"Just make sure everything is short and sweet. No one likes long speeches," cautioned Mrs. Copeland.

"Maybe we can just say their first and last name and what department of the Armed Forces they have served in. Then we can have students read some short stories or poems they wrote, thanking the veterans for their service," Kaitlyn suggested.

Annabelle and Kaitlyn were cooking with gas as they brainstormed good ideas together.

"Then the Chorus can sing some patriotic songs! I have a whole list of them." Annabelle held up a sheet of paper.

"I also think Mrs. Mitchell or Mr. Jefferson will want to give some kind of welcome address before the introductions," Kaitlyn said, and Mrs. Copeland and Annabelle quickly agreed.

Annabelle rearranged her notes to insert that item in her outline in its proper place. The planning session was going really well. After a while they had all their thoughts and ideas down on paper.

The next day Annabelle and Kaitlyn went to school early to meet with Mrs. Mitchell and the other students in the planning group. Mrs. Mitchell didn't include the whole class because she always said that "too many cooks spoil the soup," and "less is more."

Mrs. Mitchell was pleased at all the students' ideas. The next thing was to have a solid outline, which included:

- Welcome address
- Statement of Purpose
- Introduction of Veterans by students
- Stories and poems of thanks
  by students
- Patriotic songs sung
  by the Melville Chorus
- Distribution of special bookmarks
  created by students

- Closing Remarks
- Special Pre-Thanksgiving Lunch for all Veterans.

All the students in the entire school had to create special stories and poems about the veterans in the days that followed.

As the meeting came to a close, Mrs. Mitchell thanked everyone for their participation, and then it was time for school to begin.

9

CLASS TRIP

As the next week came and went, the day of the class trip to the Veterans Recreational Center finally arrived. Most of the students were excited about meeting actual Veterans and learning more about them.

A few students such as Kara and Victoria were a little shy. Kara was the quietest girl in the class and rarely spoke to anyone. But who would have thought that Victoria, such an outgoing student, would have a problem talking to adults? It seemed as if Mrs. Mitchell picked up on this situation quickly and then decided to break the class up into pairs as they spoke with each veteran.

Kaitlyn and Kara ended up being partners and Annabelle was partners with Victoria. Each student had a clipboard and the list of questions they came up with last week in their groups. Annabelle was a little concerned for Victoria and took this opportunity to speak seriously with her again.

"So Victoria, are you all right?" Annabelle asked in concern. "You look a little scared, as if you just saw a ghost."

"I'm not a fan of old people—they give me the creeps," Victoria admitted.

"What's wrong with old people, Victoria? They're human beings just like you and me, except they've lived a lot longer."

"I know that, but they're old. Ever since my grandma died, I haven't liked being around any old people. I just get a little nervous, that's all," Victoria explained.

It all made sense now. Annabelle could definitely relate to Victoria and her feelings.

"When my grandma died two years ago, I felt really sad," said Annabelle. "I really cried a lot because I missed her so much. I also felt bad for my grandpa because he had to go into a nursing home so someone else could take care of him."

"I'm so sorry to hear that, Annabelle. So what did you do to feel better?"

"My mom told me to always think about the happy times we shared together," said Annabelle. "She also told me that my grandma is in a better place now without pain. Thinking about that makes me smile," Annabelle said.

"I guess that's a good way to think

about it. I think I'll take your advice," Victoria said and smiled.

Annabelle was happy that she was really making a breakthrough with Victoria. Maybe a deeper friendship bond could form between them. Only time would tell.

Annabelle and Victoria were assigned to a little old lady who was sitting in a wheelchair. Her name was Emma McNeil, and she was a nurse who had served in the Army. She was very feisty and well-spoken. Victoria was actually starting to warm up to her as she asked her questions.

Annabelle thought Emma was funny and witty in her responses to each question. Annabelle and Victoria both enjoyed interviewing Emma. They were almost sad to leave. Before they left, they also went around and passed out the spe-

cial thank-you cards they had made for each veteran.

After the students returned to school, the school day was pretty much over. They had just spent about three hours on their trip and enjoyed it. Mrs. Mitchell told them they would do a wrap-up tomorrow and talk about their experiences.

Annabelle and Kaitlyn were on their way to Drama Club after school when they noticed Victoria standing off to the side in the hallway.

"Hey, Kaitlyn, let's invite Victoria to walk with us to Drama Club," Annabelle suggested.

"I guess we could—her attitude has been a little better these days," Kaitlyn said, although she wasn't too sure.

"Hey, Victoria, come walk with us to Drama Club!" Annabelle called to her.

Victoria was shocked to see that Kaitlyn was okay with that. She always thought Kaitlyn didn't like her, which was sort of true. But what Victoria didn't see was that she was changing for the better, making others want to be with her.

"Okay, girls, I'll be right there." Victoria hurried to catch up with them.

Once they arrived at the auditorium, they walked in and sat down with the other students. They all wondered where Mrs. Phillips was because she had not arrived yet.

"I wonder where Mrs. Phillips is—she's never late," Kaitlyn said.

"Maybe she forgot about Drama Club today. I guess I'll have to take over," Tyler said, wanting to take charge.

"You wouldn't even know what to do," said Victoria. "I'd be a better fit to take over the class. I could lead everyone in more improvisations!"

"That would certainly be fun!" Annabelle said. Everyone else seemed to agree.

They started laughing and playing around in the auditorium. Just then, everyone heard loud gobbling noises as if someone were trying to make turkey sounds. They all turned around to see who was making those noises.

To their surprise, Mrs. Phillips came out on stage in a turkey costume and pretended to be a talking turkey. As she walked around, the class began to laugh. Mrs. Phillips eventually settled everyone down in her turkey talking voice.

"Today, we're going to have some fun with Pilgrims, Native Americans, and talking turkeys! Everyone will pick a name out of a hat with a number on it. Then you will find all the ones and make a group, find all the twos and make a group, and find all the threes and make a group. You can begin now," Mrs. Phillips instructed.

The students did exactly what Mrs. Phillips said. When they separated into their groups, they did silly improvisations with a Thanksgiving Day theme. All the groups did a great job and had a fun time.

A lightbulb went off in Annabelle's head. She thought this activity was very meaningful as well as funny. After class, she immediately went up to Mrs. Phillips to share her idea.

"Mrs. Phillips, I was in the planning group for the Veterans Thanksgiving Celebration, and I think it would be a great idea to include some of these very funny Thanksgiving skits to the program!" Annabelle said with excitement.

"I think that would be a great idea too, but won't you have to clear this idea with Mrs. Mitchell first?" Mrs. Phillips said.

"Oh, of course! But I have a strong feeling that Mrs. Mitchell will love it! We can perform the skits on the stage while the veterans are eating their special Thanksgiving meal," Annabelle said, imagining the fun they would all have.

"It's okay with me if everything is approved. I think that's a great idea!"

That's all Annabelle needed to know. She knew exactly what to do next.

10

VETERANS THANKSGIVING CELEBRATION

Just as Annabelle expected, Mrs. Mitchell loved the idea of the Drama Club performing the Thanksgiving skits. She thought a little humor would be a great way to end the celebration as well as include Mrs. Phillips and the Drama Club on the program.

Mrs. Mitchell's students talked about their class trip to the Veterans Recreational Center yesterday, and everyone had a lot of terrific experiences and stories to share with one another.

Tyler began by telling everyone about how he and his partner, Caleb, interviewed a seventy-eight-year-old man who had fought in the Vietnam War. The veteran said he was happy to get out alive, but many of his friends didn't.

Kaitlyn told how she and her partner, Kara, had interviewed a woman who was fifty-eight years old. She was a Hospital Corpsman in the Navy. Kaitlyn said she was very friendly and told them that afterwards she received a degree in teaching and became a substitute teacher.

Barry and his partner, David, interviewed a sixty-year-old man who was a pilot in the Gulf War. He said that he still had his own personal plane that he flew from time to time.

Annabelle and Victoria shared their experience with Emma, the feisty nurse who had served in the Army.

The stories and experiences all the students had to share were priceless. It was a valuable field trip they would remember for years to come.

The day finally came for the Veterans Thanksgiving Celebration. The whole school wore variations of the colors red, white, and blue in their clothing. All the veterans were brought into the gymnasium because that was the biggest space in the school.

Drummers were playing some marching music as they paraded in. The veterans took their seats in chairs arranged in two rows across the stage.

Mr. Jefferson had set up the Military Color Guard from the nearby Veterans Association to come for the beginning of the program that was held in the morning. They were very serious as they marched to the center of the gymnasium.

They held the American flag, the state flag, and a lot of other flags as they led everyone in "The Pledge of Allegiance" and "The Star Spangled Banner." Afterwards, the whole school sat in amazement at the display of it all.

Mr. Jefferson gave the initial Welcome

Address and the Statement of Purpose. He kept his speeches really short. For the rest of the program, the students did everything. The presenters read very short stories and poems. The last poetry reader was Annabelle. She dedicated her poem to her grandpa and all the other brave veterans on the stage. Her poem read like this:

Veterans

Veterans are very special
They really, really are.
They have helped protect our country
From enemies near and far.

Army, Navy, Coast Guard, Marines
And the Air Force too,
Make up the five Armed
    Service branches.
Each of them is tried and true.

Men and women working together
    to achieve some common goals,

Which are peace, security,
   protection and help
For our country as a whole.

So today we truly salute you
For the thorough work you've done.
Your courage through hard times,
Your bravery will not be undone.
Each of you is Number One!

After Annabelle's final poem, the audience stood and clapped for all the veterans. Mrs. Mitchell went to the podium and gave the closing remarks, talking about the trip to the Veterans Recreational Center.

She mentioned how the students bonded with some of the brave men and women who had served our country. She talked about the awesome learning experience the students took away from this Social Studies unit.

And lastly, she spoke of all the hard work the students had put into this project and this celebration, and how very proud she was of each and every one of them. All the students were very proud to be a part of this wonderful celebration of veterans right in their very own school.

The next and final part of the celebration was the lunch that was prepared for all the veterans. The P.T.A. had the lunch provided by a food service. The presenters walked their relatives into the auditorium and sat them at special tables.

During lunch, the Drama Club presented a very funny skit called "Thanksgiving Day," which made the audience laugh. They had talking turkeys, Pilgrims, and Native Americans. This was a fictional story that Mrs. Phillips actually wrote herself! The audience really enjoyed watching the entire performance.

This would be a day that Annabelle would never forget. And to think, the very idea for this program came from Annabelle herself.

Her idea certainly made a lot of people happy, which is what Annabelle tried to do each and every day.

ANNABELLE'S DISCUSSION CORNER

1. In chapter one, Mrs. Mitchell was planning a unit on the veterans of this country. Do you know a family member or friend who is a veteran or on active duty? If so, in what branch do they serve? How many years have they served?

Make sure to thank them for their service.

2. In chapter three, Mrs. Phillips does a speech and song from a play. Have you ever seen a special play or performance with singing, acting, and dancing? If so, what was the name of the show? Write a few sentences about it and share your thoughts with a friend.

3. Have you ever stood up for a friend and spoken your mind to defend them? If so, write about what happened.

Don't forget to read the entire Amazing Annabelle Chapter Book Series!

Please visit our website: amazingannabelle.com for free teacher/student ELA resources to use in your classroom or at home. Thank you!

ABOUT THE AUTHOR

 Linda Taylor has been teaching students for over 25 years. She enjoys connecting with students on many levels. She also loves writing poetry. Linda lives on Long Island, New York.

ABOUT THE ILLUSTRATOR

 Kyle Horne has a B.A. in Visual Communications from S.U.N.Y. Old Westbury College in New York. Kyle has displayed his artwork in many local libraries. He lives on Long Island.